NEW YORK'S BRAVEST

by Mary Pope Osborne

paintings by Steve Johnson & Lou Fancher

Dragonfly Books  **New York**

A Historical Note

In the mid-nineteenth century, several thousand volunteer firefighters dragged wagons and hoses through the streets of New York, putting out countless fires in the city's wooden buildings and wharves. In 1848, a fictionalized version of one of those firefighters began appearing on the Broadway stage, performing larger-than-life heroic acts. The character was loosely based on a real-life firefighter named Mose Humphreys. Stories of the fictional Mose were soon told in newspapers, books, and more plays. In 1915, historian Herbert Asbury included many Mose legends in two collections of stories about old New York. In this book, I have drawn from the old stories and from my own imagination to add a new chapter to the Mose legend.

Mose was America's first urban folk hero. He represents the courage and strength of firefighters throughout history. Never was that courage and strength on greater display than on September 11, 2001. As workers fled the burning World Trade Center towers, New York's firefighters rushed toward the danger. Hundreds gave their lives to save others. Their extraordinary actions provide an example of all that's best in America.

—*Mary Pope Osborne*
August 2002

All rights reserved. Published in the United States by Dragonfly Books, an imprint of Random House Children's Books, a division of Random House, Inc., New York. Originally published in hardcover in the United States by Alfred A. Knopf, an imprint of Random House Children's Books, a division of Random House, Inc., New York, in 2002.

Dragonfly Books with the colophon is a registered trademark of Random House, Inc.

Visit us on the Web! www.randomhouse.com/kids

Educators and librarians, for a variety of teaching tools, visit us at www.randomhouse.com/teachers

Library of Congress Cataloging-in-Publication Data
Osborne, Mary Pope.
New York's bravest / by Mary Pope Osborne ; paintings by Steve Johnson and Lou Fancher.
    p.   cm.
Summary: Tells of the heroic deeds of the legendary New York firefighter Mose Humphreys.
ISBN 978-0-375-82196-7 (trade) — ISBN 978-0-375-92196-4 (lib. bdg.) — ISBN 978-0-375-83841-5 (pbk.)
[1. Firefighters—Fiction. 2. New York (N.Y.)—Fiction.] I. Johnson, Steve, ill. II. Fancher, Lou, ill. III. Title.
PZ7.O81167 Ne 2002
[E]—dc21
2002000455

MANUFACTURED IN CHINA
12 11 10 9 8

To the memory of the
343 New York City firefighters
who gave their lives to save others
on September 11, 2001.

"Fire! Fire! Turn out! Turn out!"

The fire bell jangled.

"Come on, boys!" said Mose.

Mose was the most famous firefighter in New York City.

Eight feet tall, Mose had hands as big as Virginia hams.

His arms were so strong he could swim the

Hudson River in two strokes.

When others ran away from danger,
Mose ran toward it.

Now Mose and his boys rolled out the pumper
and headed for the smoke billowing in the sky.

They ran past horse stables and wooden shanties.

They ran past newsboys crying, "Papers, one penny!"

They ran past oystermen, roosters, and ragmen.

Suddenly they came to a halt.

A horse-drawn trolley was stuck on the tracks, blocking their way!

"I'll take care of it, boys!" said Mose.

He lifted the crowded car into the air.
Then he set it down gently and raced on.

When Mose got to the burning tenement, a woman rushed forward.

"Help!" she screamed. "My baby's in there!"

Mose climbed a ladder to the third floor.

He hacked the wood with his ax and wedged his body inside.

Moments later he appeared, coughing and covered with soot.

"He's alone!" the mother cried. "Where's my baby!"

As Mose started down the ladder, it caught fire.

But Mose leapt through the air and landed on his feet.

Then he reached in his hat and pulled out a baby!

"Thank you! Thank you!" the mother cried.

"Just doing my duty, ma'am," said Mose.

The mother baked Mose all the pies he could eat.

To show their thanks, folks always gave Mose food and drink—

barrels of cider and coffee, bushels of oysters and potatoes, mountains of beans 'n eggs.

Ragmen gave him their least ragged clothes.

Shoeshine boys shined his boots.

Everyone knew if they ever needed help, they could count on Mose.

For years and years, Mose ran uptown and downtown, east and west, putting out fires in tenements, mansions, factories, and stores.

One night the fire bell rang. "Fire! Fire!" An eerie glow lit up the sky.

Mose and his boys pulled out the pumper and raced to the piers.

A fire in a hotel near the Hudson was roaring out of control.

All night Mose ran in and out of the building, rescuing bankers,
bakers, shoemakers, dressmakers, preachers, and politicians.
The hotel burned to ashes, but all the people inside were saved.

As the sun came up, Mose's boys packed up to leave.

"Wait a minute," one said. "Where's Mose?"

The firefighters looked around. They all stared at the
burned-out hotel. They grew silent.

"I know," one said finally. "He must've jumped in the river."

"Yeah, that's it," said another. "He must've swam to Jersey."

"Yeah, I bet he's havin' a big plate of beans 'n eggs right now."

"Yeah, beans 'n eggs. We'll see him tomorrow."

"Yeah."

But no one ever saw Mose again.

It wasn't long before the rumors started—

"Didja hear? Mose is driving a mule team in the Dakotas."

"Mose is mining gold in California."

"Mose is working in Washington for President Lincoln!"

For a long time, folks speculated on Mose's whereabouts.
Then one night, at the firehouse over a game of checkers,
an old-timer put the matter to rest.

"You know what?" he said. "Mose ain't any of them places.
Truth is, Mose is right here."

"He's marchin' with us in our parades.
He's kickin' up his heels at our fancy dances.
He's skating by moonlight on the ice pond in the park.

And whenever we climb our ladders toward
a blazing sky, he climbs with us."

"Whenever we save folks, he saves them, too.
You see, that firefighter—he'll never leave us.
He's the very spirit of New York City."